Poems from the Caribbean by **Moni**

Paintings by **Frané Less**

Not a **C**opper **P**enny in **M**e **H**ouse

Wordsong / **B**oyds **M**ills **P**ress

CONTENTS

We whitewash everything,
fences and houses,
tree trunks and stones.
Christmas is coming.

Grandpa kills a pig.
Grandma cures the ham,
soaks fruits in rum
to make her Christmas pudding.

We pick ripe sorrel
to make a red wine drink.
Bleeding hearts are in bloom.
Christmas is coming.

John Canoe dancers,
dancing through the streets
in scary costumes sing,
"Christmas is coming."

Raggedy costumes in a collage of colors,
metals and tin cans hanging,
John Canoe dancers
at Christmastime
whirl down the road.

Masks like devils or horses' heads,
waving pitchforks and sticks,
John Canoe dancers
jig down the road
to their fife and drums.

Watching them from a distance,
their clanging comes closer.
One lunges at me!
I run screaming from
the John Canoe dancers.

Roadside peddlers,
their tangerines strung on strings,
wait under bamboo lean-tos,
call out to passersby.

"Fresh fiiish,
sweet mangoes off me tree!
Nice ripe tangerines, Man,
yellow like the sun."

Roadside peddlers
holding up guineps
hurry to the windows
of buses and cars.

"This bunch sweeter!
You must try mine, Ma'am!"
and beam when they sell
even one bunch.

"Chil', me stone broke," Grandma sighs.
"Not a copper penny in me house.
Go tell Maas Charles at the corner shop
I want to trust a pound of codfish
and two pounds of rice.
I'll pay him when the produce dealer
buys me dried pimento crop in season."

Maas Charles never says no.
He knows everyone in the village
by their first names.
He scoops from his bin, weighs and wraps,
adds to his credit sheet on the wall
a new amount under Grandma's name.

Grandma always says,
"Thank God for Maas Charles."

Monday mornings in the village
housewives and maids
separate white and colored clothes
washing the white ones first,
spreading them on the grass
or mounds of stones
to bleach in the sun.

All morning long
they splash water
wetting the white clothes
until they glisten brighter and whiter
than the cotton plants,
dazzling our eyes
with their whiteness.

I'm off to the paddock,
running barefoot in the dew
with my Grandpa.

Grandpa pulling on the udders
fills his pail
with foaming milk.

Sipping warm milk,
I get a white mustache
just like Grandpa's.

Ready
to wash dishes after meals
I can't find
a bump of soap in the house.

Grandma says,
"Come Chil', let's go look
in the field and get
some velvet leaves for soap today."

We gather a bunch.
I use those leaves
like a soapy cloth
and scrub our dishes shining clean.

I watch clouds darken.
Lightning zigzags across the skies.
Winds strengthen with every gust
breaking branches from the trees.

I tremble when roofs
lift off houses and a cloudburst of rain
makes a galloping river
carrying everything away.

I peep through the shutters
wishing the rains would stop,
anxious to be a barefoot pirate
gathering floating treasures.

Today I walked home from school
through mud puddles.
I wiped my shoes clean.
Now all the shine's gone.

I like my shoes shiny
like my friend Cindy's.
There's no way poor Grandma
can buy me store polish.

But I know a way
to make leather glisten.
I blacken my shoes
with a red hibiscus.

I rub till they shine
like new patent leathers,
brighter than Cindy's
on Sunday morning.

My teacher, Miss Zettie, says,
"Children, we can't breathe in here.
Come on! We're going
under the breadfruit tree!"

We leave the one room schoolhouse
these hot days in June
for the breeze outdoors
below blue skies.

Reciting our lessons
in singsong fashion,
we hear twittering birds
recite theirs, too.

Early Saturday morning
the market bus is a moving farm
going into Kingston Town,
baskets in the aisle
bursting with breadfruits,
coconuts bumping against jackfruits,
passion fruits sitting on pumpkins,
roll with the bus along country roads.

Louder than chickens cackling,
louder than ducks quacking over a turkey's gobble,
women's chatter and laughter
make Rufus, the bus driver, shout,
"For God's sake, you noise splitting me head."
He steps on the gas, swerves the bus,
pitching women from side to side.

Crossing their hearts they zip those lips.

Sunday is Grandpa's free day.
"Thank you, God," I hear him say.
"This is my day for you.
No work in the fields today."

Sitting in his high back chair,
he doesn't know I hear
him struggle to read his Bible,
counting words in droning pairs.

Grandma nags, and he speaks out.
"Woman! You blind? Don't you see
I'm talking to me God?
For his sake, just leave me be."

Walking three miles
each Sunday morning
Nana goes to church
carrying her Sunday shoes
like a treasure.

Walking barefoot
on hard rocky roads
the soles of her feet
cracked and toughened
wear better than leather.

Walking faster
she stubs her toe hard.
Hugging her shoes
Nana says, "Thank you, God,
it wasn't me Sunday shoes."

We swim like the whales,
racing giant waves
to beat them ashore.

We toss and catch balls,
laughing when we fall
on the warm sands.

We feast on fried fish,
wash it down with fresh juice
from the coconut tree.

Stretched out on mats
we rest and doze,
listening to the waves.

I'm part of the bustle
in the village square.
It's Christmas Eve again.
Grand Market Night is here.

I jingle my pennies
for sparklers and a treat.
I hope to find a trinket
when I buy my lucky box.

Drummers and fifers play.
People shop and laugh and dance.
We light our sparklers.
Hurrah for Grand Market Night!

Text copyright © 1993 by Monica Gunning
Illustrations copyright © 1993 by Frane´ Lessac

Published by Wordsong
Boyds Mills Press, Inc.
A Highlights Company
815 Church Street
Honesdale, Pennsylvania 18431
Printed in China

Publisher Cataloging-in-Publication Data
Gunning, Monica.
  Not a copper penny in me house : poems from the Caribbean / by Monica Gunning :
paintings by Frané Lessac. 1st ed.
[32]p. : col. ill. ; cm.
Summary : Poems relating to life in the Caribbean.
ISBN 1-56397-793-1
1. Caribbean poetry (English) Juvenile literature. 2. Children's poetry.
[1. Caribbean poetry (English) Poetry.] 1. Lessac, Frané, ill. II. Title.
811.54 dc20   1993
Library of Congress Catalog Card Number 92-61631

First Boyds Mills Press paperback edition, 1999
Book designed by Joy Chu
The text of this book is set in 16-point Goudy Old Style.
The illustrations are done in gouache.

10 9 8 7 6 5

For Myra Cohn Livingston—M.G.

For my grandparents—F.L.